This book
belongs to

....

....

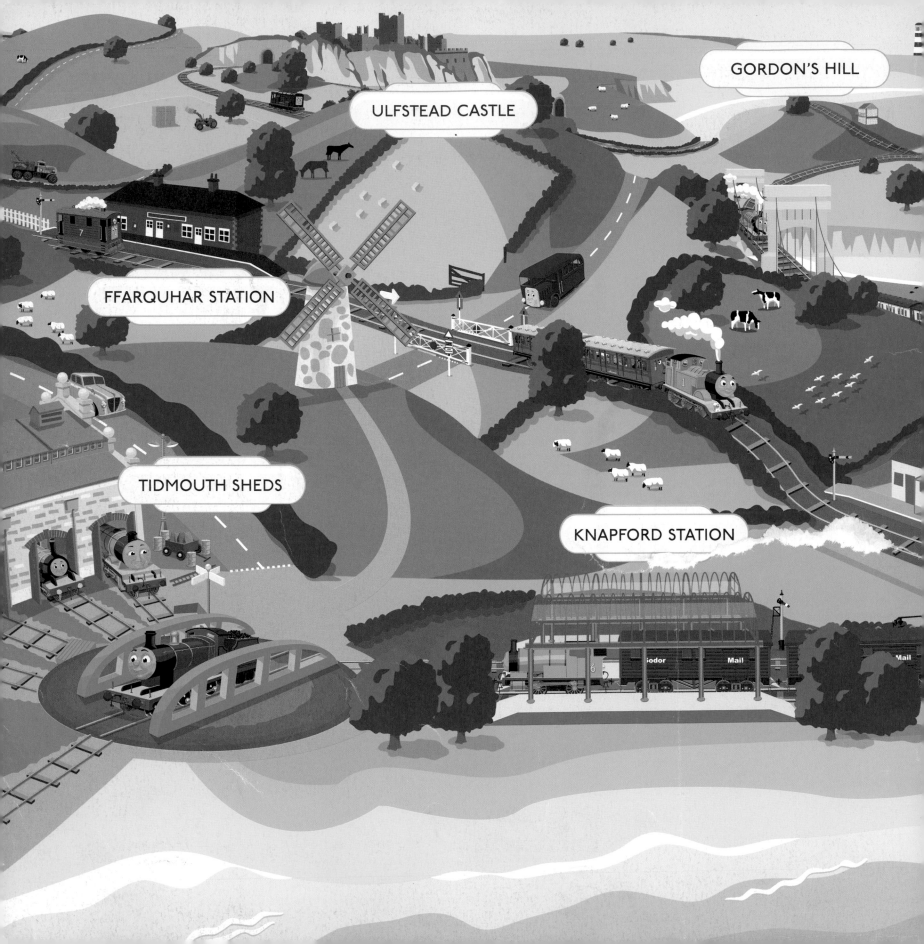

GORDON'S HILL

ULFSTEAD CASTLE

FFARQUHAR STATION

TIDMOUTH SHEDS

KNAPFORD STATION

BRENDAM DOCKS

CHINA CLAY PITS

DRYAW STATION

THE ISLAND OF SODOR

EGMONT
We bring stories to life

First published in Great Britain in 2015 by Egmont UK Limited
The Yellow Building, 1 Nicholas Road, London W11 4AN

Written by Joseph Marriott and Jane Riordan
Designed by Martin Aggett
Illustrated by Robin Davies
Map illustration by Dan Crisp

Thomas the Tank Engine & Friends ™

CREATED BY BRITT ALLCROFT

ISBN 978 1 4052 7605 4
59059/1

Printed in Italy

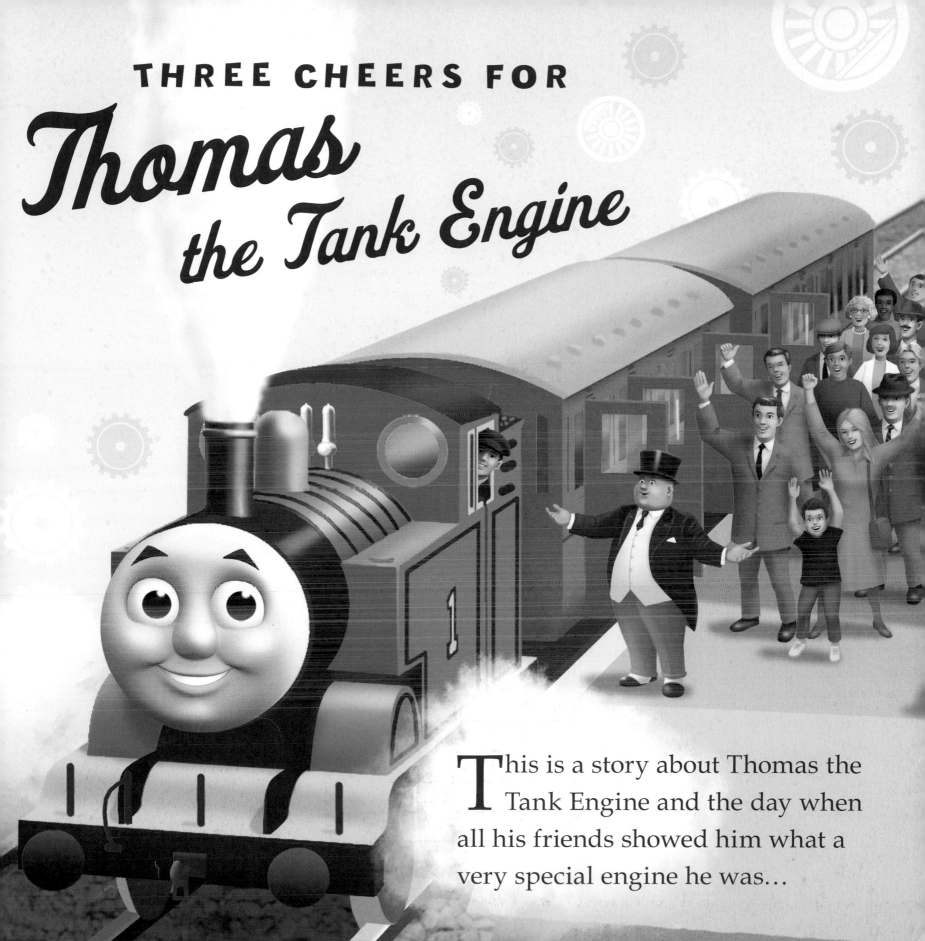

THREE CHEERS FOR
Thomas
the Tank Engine

This is a story about Thomas the Tank Engine and the day when all his friends showed him what a very special engine he was…

One sunny day on the Island of Sodor, Thomas was running late.

The next day was no better.
Thomas was late to be coupled up to Annie and Clarabel...

late delivering
goods trucks...

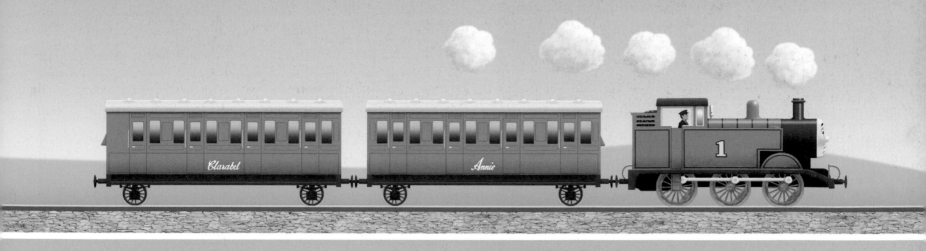

late shunting trucks...

...and late to the Washdown at the end of the day.

It was the same story all week.

Normally Thomas loved to race with his friend Bertie the Bus but on this day Thomas was too tired and his wheels were too sore to rush about.

"Not today, Bertie," said Thomas.

That night, Thomas puffed back to the Sheds, very slowly and very sadly.

Everyone was worried about Thomas. He was normally such a **cheerful little engine**. Nobody liked seeing him so sad.

"I remember when I had my **old, rusty pipes**," said James. "I felt so slow and tired. I used to get out of breath, even on the shortest journey."

So the Engines decided to talk
to The Fat Controller to see
what could be done.

"Thomas' wheels are **rusty and worn,**"
The Fat Controller said, "We'll give him a
special day with new paint, new wheels
and a **surprise party** to celebrate!"

"With new wheels, Thomas
might be *faster* than you, Bertie,"
teased Emily.

"**Never!**"

tooted Bertie.

The next day The Fat Controller went to see Thomas.

"Today," he said, "you won't be pulling Annie and Clarabel. I'm sending you to the **Sodor Steamworks**."

"I understand," thought Thomas, sadly. "I'm not good enough to pull coaches. I'm not a Really Useful Engine."

And he **puffed** off to the Steamworks feeling very sorry for himself.

But at the Steamworks Thomas was given a smart **new coat of paint...**

...his dome was **polished...**

...his buffers were **buffed...**

...and he was given **brand new, shiny wheels!**

"Perhaps The Fat Controller thinks I can be a Useful Engine after all," said Thomas.

"I certainly do," laughed The Fat Controller, arriving to inspect the work. "You look ready for your party."

"My party, Sir?" exclaimed Thomas.

Thomas was about to puff off to his party at Knapford Station when Bertie pulled up next to him.

"Let's race to the party!" Bertie said. "It's time to test out those special new wheels."

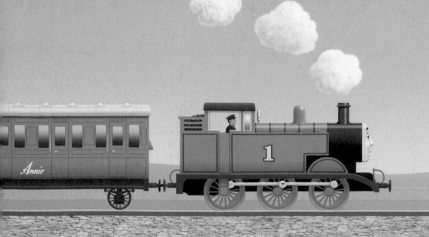

Bertie pulled away **more quickly** than Thomas and took the lead.

But Thomas' new wheels were turning **faster** and **faster** and **faster**.

He was catching up.

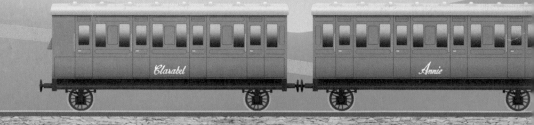

And when Bertie stopped to let some ducks cross the road, **Thomas overtook him!**

"Three cheers for Thomas!" said The Fat Controller, as they arrived first at the party.

"Hip hip hooray!
Hip hip hooray!
Hip hip hooray!"

"I just couldn't keep up with those new wheels," Bertie said as he pulled up.

It was a **wonderful party**! All Thomas' friends congratulated him on winning the race. Then they admired his new coat of paint and his shiny new wheels.

"Peep! Peep!"
Thomas tooted happily.

"I'm happy Thomas is back to his old self," said James to Bertie that night.

"Yes, it was fun racing him," smiled Bertie. "But next time he might not be so lucky!"

But Thomas didn't hear any of this,
because he was already fast asleep.

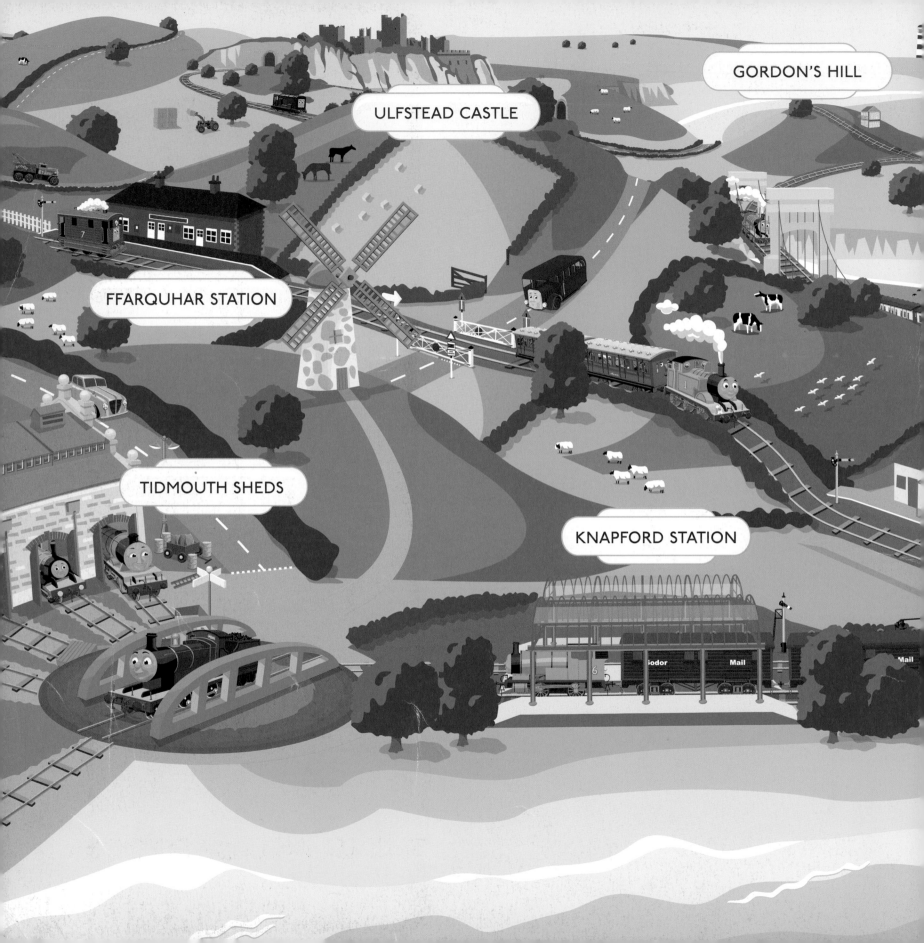

GORDON'S HILL

ULFSTEAD CASTLE

FFARQUHAR STATION

TIDMOUTH SHEDS

KNAPFORD STATION

About the author

The Reverend W. Awdry was the creator of 26 little books about Thomas and his famous engine friends, the first being published in 1945. The stories came about when the Reverend's two-year-old son Christopher was ill in bed with the measles. Awdry invented stories to amuse him, which Christopher then asked to hear time and time again. And now for 70 years, children all around the world have been asking to hear these stories about Thomas, Edward, Gordon, James and the many other Really Useful Engines.

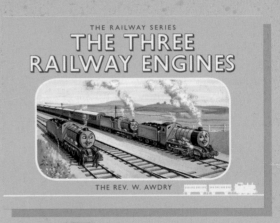

THE RAILWAY SERIES
THE THREE RAILWAY ENGINES

THE REV. W. AWDRY

The Three Railway Engines, first published in 1945.

The Reverend Awdry with some of his readers at a model railway exhibition.